For my mother, friend and mentor. —M.E.W.

*For my mother and father who have taught me strength
and determination and who passionately
encouraged me to follow my dreams, and most
important of all, my husband Rick, my best friend, who
has always believed in me.* —T.C.K.

Text © 1998 by Mary E. Whitcomb
Illustrations © 1998 by Tara Calahan King. All rights reserved.

Book design by Lucy Nielsen.
Typeset in Berkeley Oldstyle and Fontesque.
The illustrations in this book were rendered in color pencils and pastels.
Printed in China.

Library of Congress Cataloging-in-Publication Data

Whitcomb, Mary E.
Odd Velvet / by Mary E. Whitcomb ;
illustrated by Tara Calahan King
p. cm.
Summary: Although she dresses differently from the other girls
and does things which are unusual, Velvet eventually teaches her
classmates that even an outsider has something to offer.
ISBN 0-8118-2004-1 (hardcover)
[1. Individuality—Fiction. 2. Schools—Fiction.]
I. King, Tara Calahan, ill. II. Title.
PZ7.W57950f 1998 [E]—dc21 98-10966 CIP
AC

Distributed in Canada by Raincoast Books
8680 Cambie Street, Vancouver, British Columbia V6P 6M9

10 9 8 7 6 5 4 3

Chronicle Books
85 Second Street, San Francisco, California 94105

www.chroniclebooks.com

Odd Velvet

by Mary E. Whitcomb ✿ illustrated by Tara Calahan King

chronicle books · san francisco

On the first day of school, Velvet's classmates brought their teacher cinnamon tea, lace handkerchiefs, and heart-shaped boxes of potpourri.

Velvet handed her teacher an egg carton filled with seven rocks, her favorite red shoelaces, and half a sparrow's egg.

Velvet was odd.

At lunchtime, Velvet not only carried a used brown paper bag, but inside of it were things like carrots and a butter sandwich. And she *ate* them.

At recess, a few of the girls noticed that Velvet was not wearing a new dress even though it was the beginning of the school year.

"Where did she come from?" they wondered out loud.

All of this strangeness did not stop after the first day of school.
In fact, it got worse.

Velvet brought in a milkweed pod for show and tell. Luckily,
three of the other girls brought in a talking doll, a wetting doll,
and a crying doll, and saved the day.

Velvet's nose was freckled, she had a pack of only eight crayons, and her sweater once belonged to her older sister. Nothing was right about Odd Velvet.

Although everyone was polite to her, no one was silly enough to pick Velvet for partner play or to walk home with her after school.

No one wanted to be different the way Velvet was different.

On the day of the school field trip, the children were laughing and calling each other by their nicknames. Someone called out . . .

"What's YOUR nickname, Velvet?"

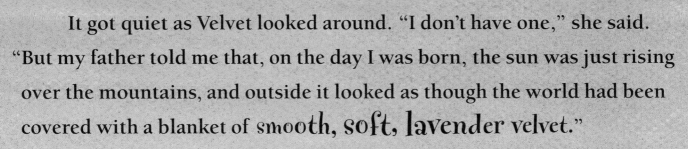

It got quiet as Velvet looked around. "I don't have one," she said. "But my father told me that, on the day I was born, the sun was just rising over the mountains, and outside it looked as though the world had been covered with a blanket of smooth, soft, lavender velvet."

A few of the boys let out a giggle, but mostly the bus fell quiet. For a moment everyone was thinking of how beautiful that morning must have been, the day Velvet was born.

The following week a school drawing contest was announced. There was no question who the winner would be. Sarah Garvey had the best markers, the biggest paint set, and more colored pencils than anyone else in the class.

When the day arrived to announce the winner, the children let Sarah sit right up front. No one was more surprised than she was when the teacher called out Velvet's name.

Velvet had drawn an apple. "It's just a piece of fruit," Sarah protested. Everyone stared at the picture. "It looks so real I would like to eat it," someone said. "It seems like you could pick it up," another child added. Sure enough, with just her eight crayons, Velvet had drawn the most beautiful apple the children had ever seen.

Little by little, the things that Velvet said, and the things that Velvet did began to make sense.

The teacher had Velvet speak for two whole days about her rock collection.

She even had ashes from a real volcano.

Still, on the day she handed out invitations to her birthday party, the whispering began.

"I bet her house is old and dark," Sarah said. The thought of going to Velvet's house made everyone feel a little uneasy.

Velvet lived in a tiny house at the end of a long road. There was no jungle gym or tether ball. Just a tall swing hanging from a big, old tree.

At the door, Velvet's mom and dad politely asked the children in. There were no birthday magicians, or wizards. Not even a clown.

But they got to turn Velvet's room into a castle. The royal subjects painted their faces and put glitter in their hair. They jumped high off the bed into a blue blanket moat.

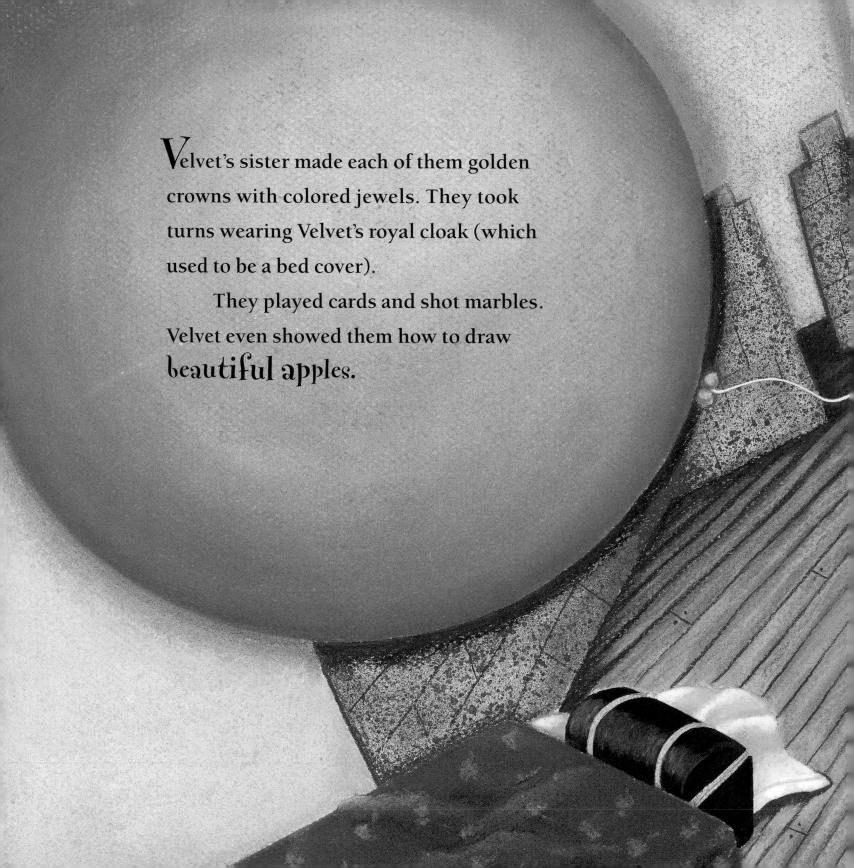

Velvet's sister made each of them golden crowns with colored jewels. They took turns wearing Velvet's royal cloak (which used to be a bed cover).

They played cards and shot marbles. Velvet even showed them how to draw beautiful apples.

On the last day of school, Velvet's classmates brought their teacher handfuls of flowers, cards that they had made, and an impressive collection of nice looking rocks.

Velvet was different.
But, maybe she wasn't so odd after all.